CLAUDIA BOLDT

W9-AKW-335

Odd Dog

WITHDRAWN

This book belongs to

- - - - - - - - - - - - - - -

American adaptation copyright © 2012 by
North-South Books Inc., New York 10016.
Copyright © Claudia Boldt 2012
The right of Claudia Boldt to be identified as the author of this work has been
asserted in accordance with the Copyright, Designs and Patents Act 1988.
First published by Random House Children's Books

All rights reserved.
No part of this book may be reproduced or utilized in any form or
by any means, electronic or mechanical, including photo-copying,
recording, or any information storage and retrieval system, without
permission in writing from the publisher.

First published in the United States in 2012 by North-South Books Inc.,
an imprint of NordSüd Verlag AG, CH-8005 Zürich, Switzerland.

Distributed in the United States in 2012 by North-South Books Inc., New York 10016.
Library of Congress Cataloging-in-Publication Data is available.
ISBN: 978-0-7358-4068-3 (trade edition)
1 3 5 7 9 · 10 8 6 4 2
Printed in China by Toppan Leefung Packaging & Printing (Dongguan)
Co., Ltd., Dongguan, P.R.C., February 2012
www.northsouth.com

For Gustav and Sebastian

3 9082 12633 9095

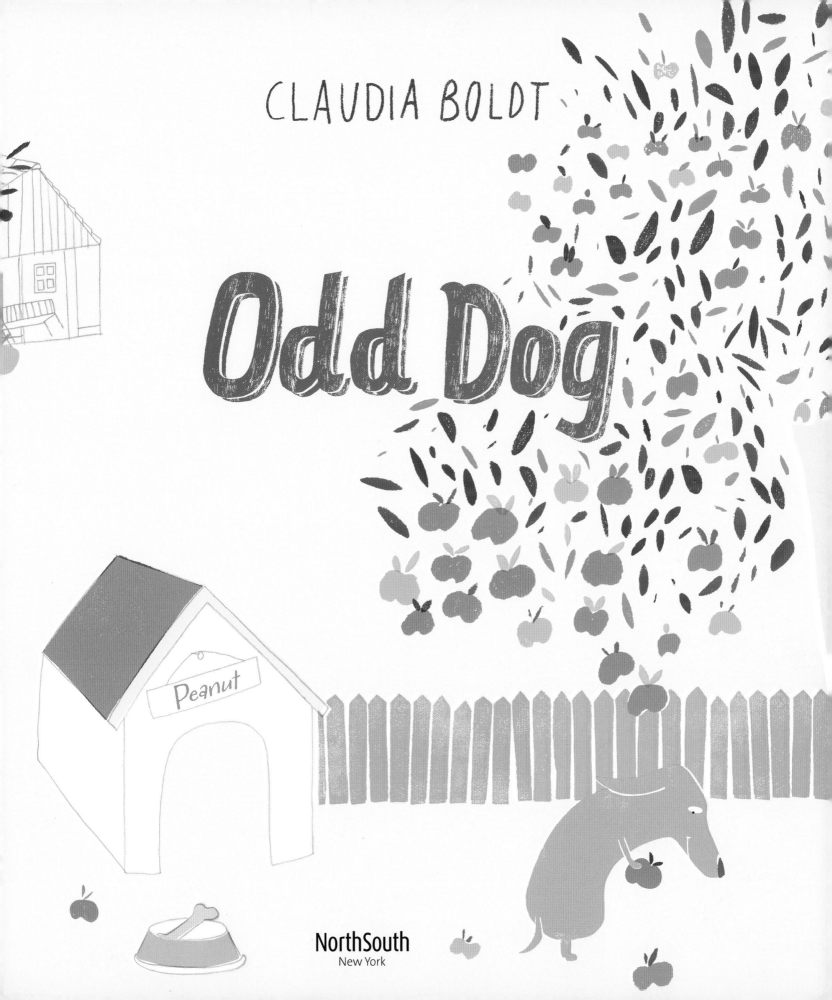

CLAUDIA BOLDT

Odd Dog

Peanut

NorthSouth
New York

Peanut was an odd dog.
Unlike all the other dogs he did not
care for bones, but he loved apples.
His apple tree was his pride and joy.

Peanut loved the apples
from his tree so much that
he was always worried
that his neighbor, Milo, was
plotting to steal them.

At night, Peanut dreamed about
his apple tree.

Sometimes he would wake up so worried
that he couldn't get back to sleep.

And sometimes he would have nightmares that Milo had found a way to steal one of the apples or—even worse—all of them.

So he counted them every morning, just to make sure.

15 16 17

One day, disaster struck!

The juiciest apple of all was just
about to fall into Milo's garden.
There was no time to lose!

WITHDRAWN

Peanut tried everything . . .

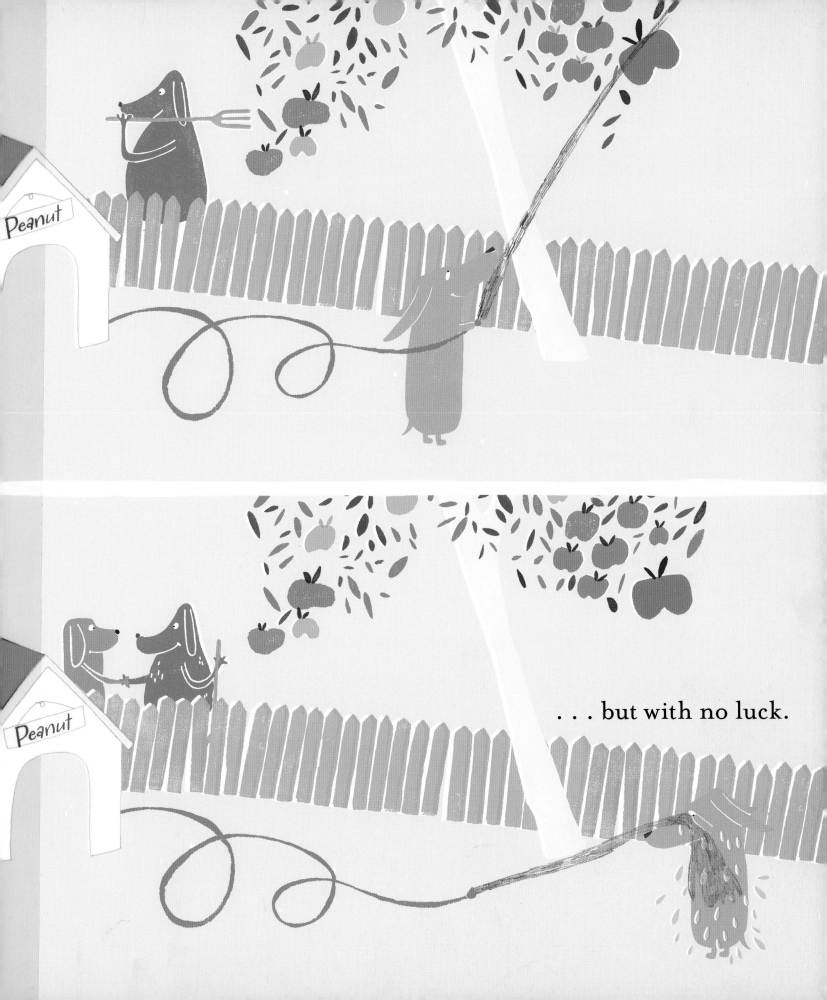

. . . but with no luck.

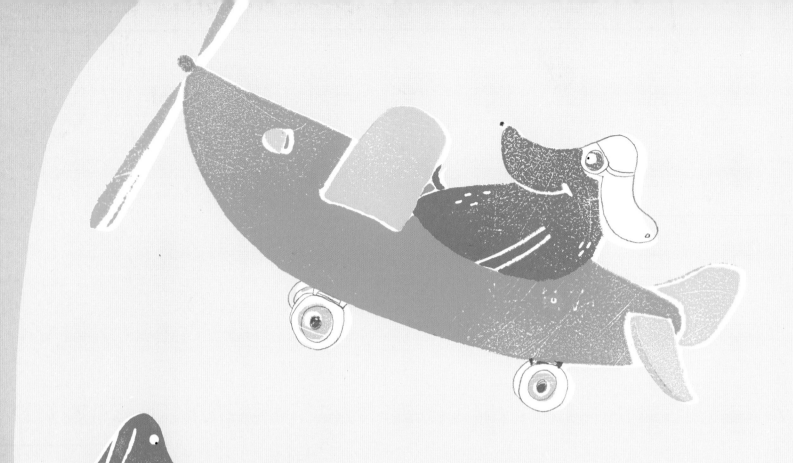

"Milo's going to get my best apple—just like he always gets everything," Peanut thought. "It's not fair!"

Peanut was feeling
dreadfully sorry for himself,
when all of a sudden . . .

noooooo!

. . . the apple fell.

Clang!

The apple landed in Milo's bowl.

But instead of eating the apple, Milo said,
"Here you go, Peanut! This apple looks
very ripe and juicy, and I know how much
you love them."
Peanut was very surprised. "Oh," he said.
"Thank you. Um . . . would you like a bite?"
"No, thank you very much," said Milo.
"I don't really like apples. I love bones."

Peanut wanted to thank Milo for returning the apple, so he invited him for a picnic.

And from that day on . . .

WITHDRAWN

. . . they were the very best of friends.